1
THE CAMERA

Max gave Felix a present on his birthday.
"I wrapped it myself," Max said.
"I can tell," said Felix.
"It's a camera," said Max.
"I can see," said Felix.
"It's just what I wanted."
"Take my picture," said Max.
"That's an idea," said Felix.

Max zipped down the sidewalk on his skateboard.

"Hold it. Hold it," said Felix.

"Hurry!" said Max.

Click.

"I got it," said Felix.

Max dusted himself off.

"We'll see," he said.

Later, Max and Felix looked at the picture.
"That isn't the picture you were
supposed to take," Max said.
"It captures the action," said Felix.
"It captures my spill," said Max.
Felix shrugged.
"Let's try something else," he said.

"Shouldn't you have both hands on the handlebars?" Felix shouted.
"Just take the picture," said Max.
CLICK.

"You waited too long," said Max.

"It shows me upside-down."

"That is the way you were," Felix said.

"Let's try something else."

Max sat very still.

"Smile," said Felix.

"I am smiling," said Max.

Felix set the timer and dashed to Max's side.

Max made room.

CLICK.

"It's perfect," said Felix.
Even Max had to agree.

2 THE PORCH

Max was building a porch.
"It doesn't look right," said Felix.
"Nonsense," said Max.
"Those steps are a little shaky," said Felix.
"You need more nails.
And one end of the porch is higher than the other."
"It takes time," said Max.
"It's not finished yet."
Felix couldn't help himself.
"A carpenter would get it right
in no time at all," he said.

"Please," said Max.
"Just go away. When it's finished,
we'll have a porch-sitting party."
"I won't hold my breath," said Felix.
And he went home to putter
in his garden.

The next morning Felix's phone rang.
"Come sit on my porch," said Max.
Felix grabbed his camera and ran straight to
Max's house.

"Ta da!" Max announced.

"It's finished."

Felix was flabbergasted.

"Really?" he said.

"I bet you've never seen a porch like it," said Max.

"You win the bet," said Felix.

Max leaned against the railing.
CLICK.

Max dusted himself off.
"I bet there will never be another porch like it,"
he said.
Felix had to agree.

3
THE
STORY

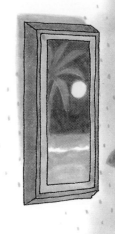

Late one summer night Max had a wicked idea.
"Would you like to hear a story?" he asked
in his most ghoulish voice.
"Hot dog!" said Felix.
"There's nothing better than a story."

"It's a story about a night
just like this night," said Max.
"Were there two friends?" Felix asked.
"There were two friends," said Max.
"Was the moon full?" Felix asked.
"The moon was full," said Max.
"Was it quiet?" Felix asked.
"It was quiet," said Max, "so quiet that the
only sound was the sound of a beating heart.
Lub-dub. Lub-dub."

"This is exciting," said Felix.
"Are you sure that that was the only sound?"
"It was the only sound," said Max.
"And it kept getting closer
and closer
and closer."
"Ooooh," said Felix.

"Do you want me to stop?" asked Max.

"Don't be silly," said Felix.

"Closer and closer came the sound," said Max.

"Lub-dub. Lub-dub."

"How close did the sound come?" asked Felix.

"Close," said Max. "Very close."

"And there weren't any other sounds?" Felix asked.

"None," said Max.

"Lub-dub. Lub-dub."

"Are you sure there were no other sounds?" Felix asked.

"Absolutely none," said Max.

"Lub-dub. Lub-dub."

CLICK.

"Heeelp!" cried Max.

Max dusted himself off.
"You scared me," he said.
"So I see," said Felix.

4

THE CATCH

Early one morning Max and Felix met at the pond.
"I bet my fishing hole is luckier than yours," said Max.
"We'll see," said Felix.
Max rowed his boat to his lucky fishing hole.
Felix rowed his boat to his lucky fishing hole.
They fished away the morning.

"Have you had any luck?" Max shouted.
"Have you?" Felix shouted back.
Just then something tugged at Max's line.
"It must be a whale!" Max shouted,
and he began to reel in his fishing line.

Just then something tugged at Felix's line.
"We'll see about that!" he said,
and he began to reel in his fishing line.

Max pulled and pulled.

Felix pulled and pulled.

Very soon Max was near the end of his fishing line.
So was Felix.

Later Felix asked a tourist to take a picture
for his photo album.
CLICK.
"Lucky catch," said the tourist.
Max and Felix had to agree.